Lucy and Seymour's Circus

Story and Illustrations by Sally O. Lee

I would like to thank Stephanie Robinson,
and the staff at BookSurge
in helping me to publish this book.
www.booksurge.com

I would also like to thank my family and
friends for their love and support.

This book is typeset in Garamond and Lucy.

www.leepublishing.net

To: Mom and Dad

One sunny morning, Lucy's mother walked in to Lucy's room and said,

"Good Morning, Lucy!
We are going to the circus today!"

Lucy groaned, "Today? Oh."

Her mother said, "I thought you were excited about going to the circus."

"I was." Lucy replied.

Lucy's mother sensed that something was wrong.
She felt Lucy's forehead and said,

"Oh, dear, it looks like you have a temperature.
I guess we will not be going to the circus today."

"But I wanted to go to the circus." said Lucy.

"I know, but we will have to go on a day when you are feeling better. I will bring you some juice and crackers. But you should rest today." replied her mother.

Lucy was very disappointed but she did as her mother told her to do.

Lucy looked at
Sydney, her dog,
and Seymour, her cat, and said,

"Oh, well, I guess we are not
going to the circus today."
Lucy frowned, and then smiled,
"But maybe, we could make
our own circus!"

Seymour, Sydney and Anabel
jumped up and down on the bed.
They knew that this was
the best idea ever.

So, they all started to
plan a circus.

"First, we need a circus tent." Lucy said.

So Lucy, Seymour, and Sydney looked around her room for a circus tent. They found a striped blanket which could be transformed in to a tent.

They threw the blanket over one of the bed posts and tied the ends of the blanket to the corners of the bed.

It was the perfect circus tent.

*L*ucy, Seymour, Sydney, and
Anabel the elephant
ventured inside the tent.

Seymour ran in to the middle of the tent.

He stretched
out his arms and shouted,

"Welcome one and all,
to Lucy and Seymour's Circus! The greatest
circus of all time! Come and get your popcorn
and root beer and enjoy the greatest show
in the world! We have elephants and lions and tight
rope walkers! You won't believe your eyes!
So take your seats and join us!"

Lucy, Anabel, and Sydney clapped their
hands and hollered
as loud as they possible could.

Seymour bowed and the show began.

It suddenly became very quiet in the tent.
You could hear a whisper.

Out of the darkness came Seymour doing his
death-defying hand stand on Anabel's back.
Anabel trotted around the ring as Seymour
twirled andspun and jumped. Seymour stood
on one hand, then on two hands, and
then he flipped in the air and landed on his feet.

Anabel shouted out a huge elephant roar
and everyone cheered.

"Yeah! Woo Hoo! That was wonderful,
Seymour! Do it again!"

So Seymour and Anabel ran around
the ring a few more times
and walked in to the darkness again.

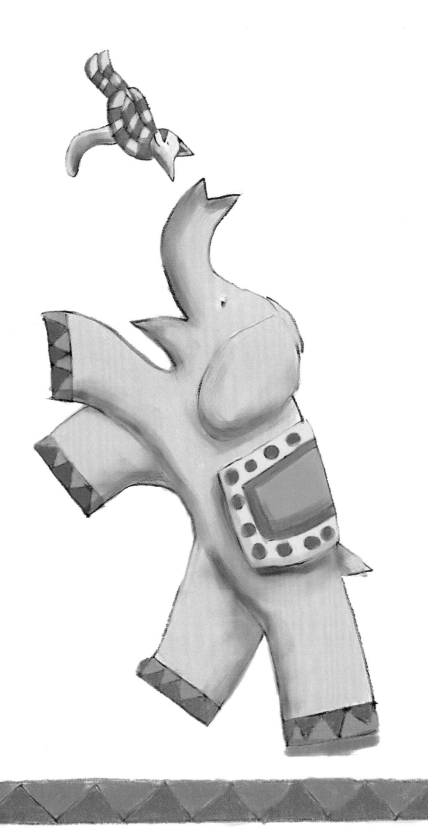

Then, Lucy appeared from the sky
swinging from a trapeze.

She swung to the right,
and she swung to the left,
and then......

Lucy hung upside down
from the trapeze bar.

The crowd gasped
with excitement.

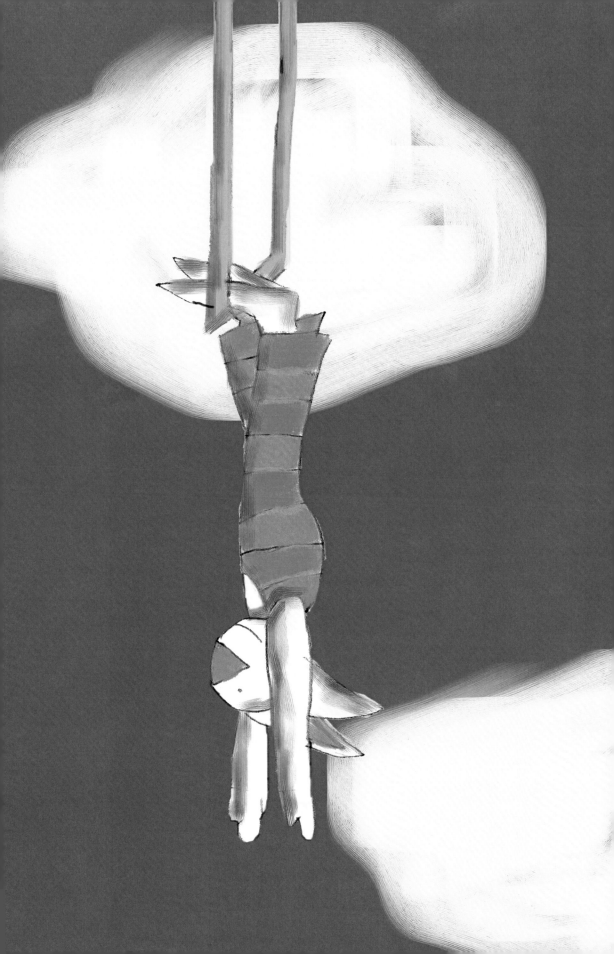

All was silent again in the big, striped tent...when suddenly Seymour reappeared again standing on the back of a fierce, furry lion.

Well, Lulu the lion was not exactly fierce but she tried really hard to look fierce. Seymour stretched Lulu's big toothed mouth wide open and stuck his head inside.

The crowd roared.

Lulu and Seymour disappeared once again in to the darkness of the big circus tent.

A single spotlight shined at the top of the tent,
and there was Seymour
riding his bike on a thin rope.

"Oooooooh." hushed the crowd.

The thin rubber wheels turned round and round...

And then, Seymour disappeared
once again in to the darkness
of the big circus tent.

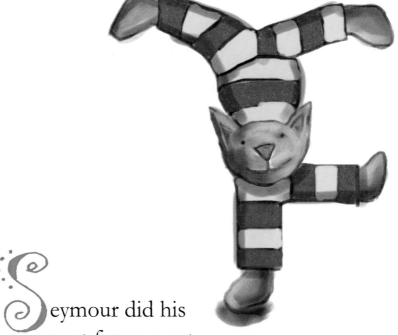

Seymour did his
most famous act
of all which
was to
balance on a
big orange ball.

Sydney

juggled

four

balls

all at

the same

time.

Lucy heard a knock at the door.

"I hear cheering and clapping in here." said her mother.

"What are you up to, Lucy?"

"Hi, Mom. We decided to have our own circus since we couldn't go to the real circus today." said Lucy.

"Oh!" said her mother. "Were there lions and elephants and tight rope walkers?"

"Yes!" exclaimed Lucy.
"And we had a trapeze artist too!"
They all giggled.

Lucy's mother felt her forehead, and Lucy was feeling better.

"Well, I am glad you had fun at the circus today.
But I think you should go to sleep now."
her mother replied.

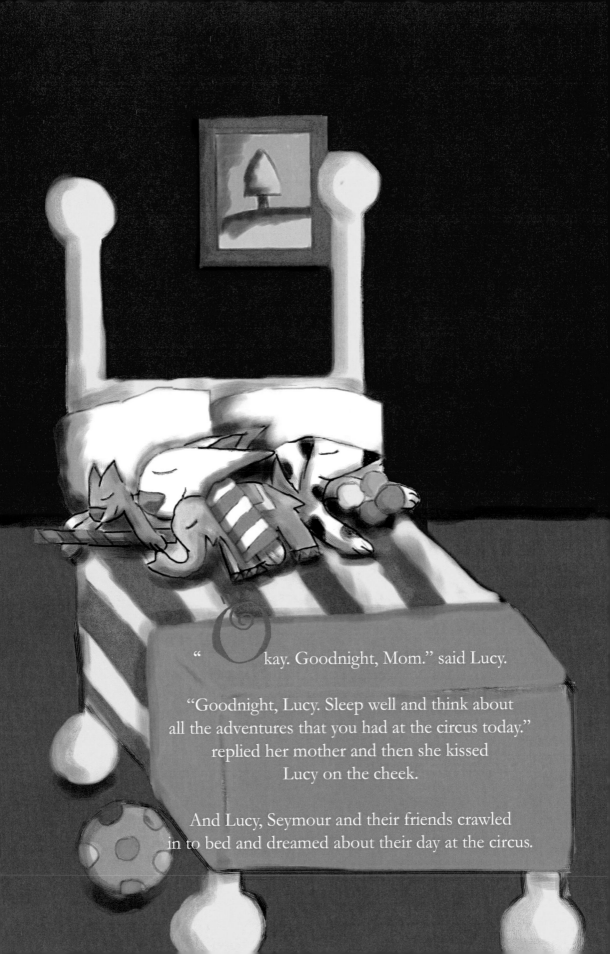

" Okay. Goodnight, Mom." said Lucy.

"Goodnight, Lucy. Sleep well and think about
all the adventures that you had at the circus today."
replied her mother and then she kissed
Lucy on the cheek.

And Lucy, Seymour and their friends crawled
in to bed and dreamed about their day at the circus.

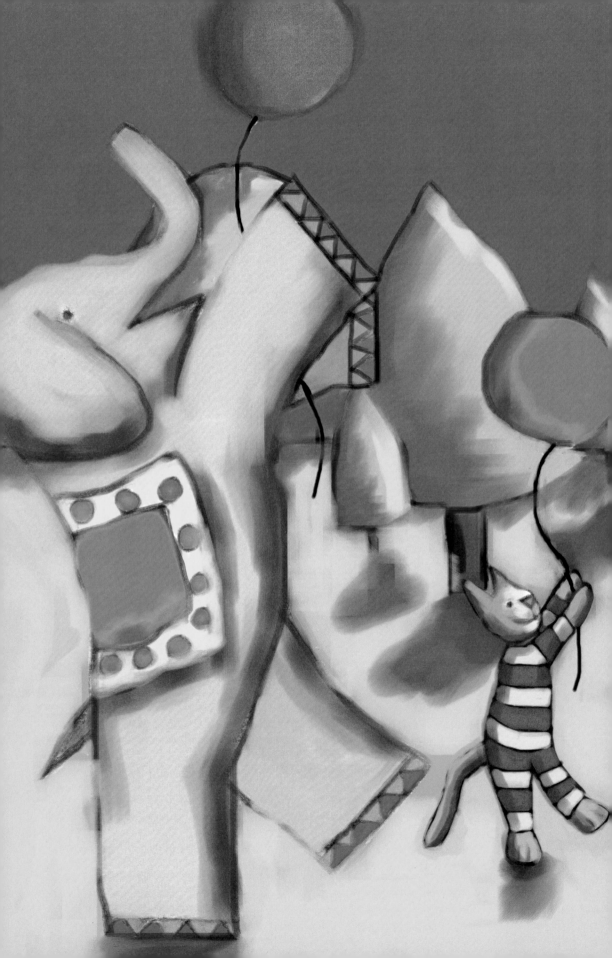